Out to Sea

By
Anne & Harlow Rockwell

Ready-to-Read

Macmillan Publishing Co., Inc.

New York

Macmillan Publishing Co., Inc.
866 Third Avenue, New York, N.Y. 10022
Collier Macmillan Canada, Ltd.
Printed in the United States of America

10   9   8   7   6   5   4   3   2   1

LIBRARY OF CONGRESS CATALOGING IN PUBLICATION DATA
Rockwell, Anne F
    Out to sea.
    (Ready-to-read)
    SUMMARY: A brother and sister are inadvertently
swept out to sea while playing in an old row boat they
have found on the beach.
    [1. Boats and boating—Fiction]   I. Rockwell, Harlow,
joint author.   II. Title.
PZ7.R5943Ou 1980   [E]   80-12520   ISBN 0–02–777620–4

TO ALL
BEETLE
CATS

Chapter One

Jeff and Kate
were picking up driftwood.
They were going to build a fire
to cook hamburgers
on the beach.
Mother and Father
were unpacking the lunch.
Suddenly Jeff and Kate
saw something.

"Look at that boat,"
said Jeff.
There was a little boat
lying among the rocks and seaweed.
It was upside down.

"Let's turn it over,"
said Kate.
The little boat was old
and the seat was broken,
but there were no holes in it
that they could see.
The little boat had been
washed onto the rocks and seaweed
in a storm.

"Let's pretend we are going
out to sea," said Kate.
"I will be the captain."
"No, I want to be the captain,"
said Jeff.
"No, I am older," said Kate.
"I will be the captain."
So she was.
Jeff and Kate played
in the little boat.
They pretended it was a big ship
and that Kate was the captain
and Jeff was the crew.

Mother and Father finished
getting the lunch ready.
Then they sat down on the beach
to wait for Jeff and Kate
to come back.

The tide was coming in.
The little waves came
closer and closer.
Mother and Father could not
see Jeff and Kate.

Jeff and Kate were busy
playing and pretending.
They did not notice
when a little wave
washed the boat off
the rocks and seaweed.

But they did notice when
a bigger wave
splashed into the boat.
They could see the rocks
on the beach,
but they could not see
the seaweed any more.
The tide had covered it very fast.

"Hey! Look at us," said Jeff.
"We are floating.
We are floating on the sea."
"Yes, that is true," said Kate.
"I think we should go back
to the beach. But how?"

The little boat had no oars,
no motor and no sail.
Jeff and Kate began
to paddle hard
with their hands.
But the boat kept floating
away from the beach
faster and faster.

Chapter Two

It was time for lunch.
Mother and Father called
Jeff and Kate,
but they did not answer.
"I will go find them," said Father.
Father walked along the beach.
He saw a pile of driftwood.
He saw a horseshoe crab shell,
a piece of old rope
and Jeff's sneakers.
But he did not see Jeff and Kate.

Suddenly he saw the little boat
floating on the sea.

He saw Jeff and Kate
sitting in it and
paddling hard with their hands.
He shouted to them,
"Come back!"
But they could not hear him.

Father took off his sneakers
and ran into the sea.
He was going to swim
to Jeff and Kate.

Mother came running.

She saw Father.

She saw Jeff and Kate.

And she saw a sign that said,

NO SWIMMING
DANGEROUS
CURRENT

She called to Father,
"Come back! Come back!
You cannot swim to them!"
It was true.
Father could feel
the dangerous current.
He could feel the tide
trying to pull him
out to sea.
He swam back while he could.

Mother and Father ran
to the car.
They drove off to get help.

The little boat floated
farther and farther
away from the beach.
A big fish jumped
beside the boat.

Then a little fish jumped
out of the blue sea
and a seagull ate it.
Jeff began to cry.
"Don't be such a baby,"
said Kate.
"Crying won't help."

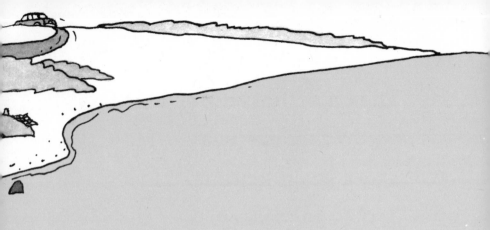

But she saw the beach far away.

She saw the car drive off.

And she began to cry, too.

Chapter Three

Mother and Father drove
to the harbor master's office
on the dock.
They told him Jeff and Kate
had floated out to sea.
The harbor master called
the Coast Guard.

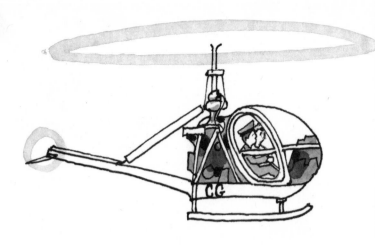

The Coast Guard sent
a helicopter and a motor boat
to look for the little boat
with Jeff and Kate in it.

As the little boat bobbed
and floated on the blue sea,
Jeff and Kate held
each other tight
and tried to stop crying.
A trickle of sea water
began to come into the boat.
The old boat had started to leak.

Chapter Four

Jeff and Kate took off
their T-shirts.
They mopped up the water
from the bottom of the boat
and wrung out the T-shirts
into the sea.
They kept mopping
and wringing,
mopping and wringing,
as the sea water came in.

Suddenly a sailboat sailed
close to them.
Jeff and Kate began to wave
and shout.
The sailboat sailed closer.

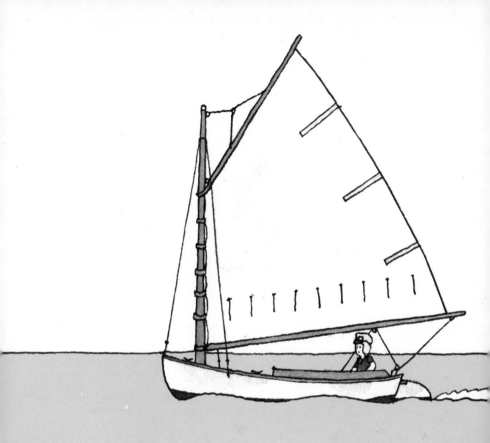

A woman was all alone in it.
Jeff and Kate said,
"We got washed out to sea.
We cannot get home."
"I will take you home,"
said the woman.
"Come aboard."
She helped Jeff
into the sailboat.
Then she helped Kate.

But when Kate stepped
into the sailboat,
the little boat tipped over
with a big splash
and bobbed and floated
upside down on the blue waves.

"Put on these life jackets,"
said the woman.
"Now lower your heads.
Ready, about!" she called.
The sail swung over their heads
and the boat turned around.

The wind came up.

The sail filled with wind.

Then the sailboat went fast.

"I feel sick to my stomach,"

said Jeff,

and he lay down.

"You must be seasick,"

said the woman.

"Sit up, and watch the water.

Watch the water move.

Then you will feel better."

Jeff did sit up

and he did feel better.

But Kate was not seasick at all.

As Jeff and Kate
and the woman sailed
toward the harbor,
the Coast Guard helicopter
flew over the sea.

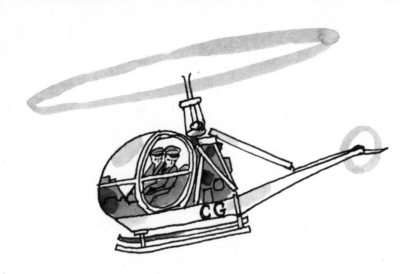

The people in the helicopter
saw the little boat.
They saw it bobbing and floating
upside down on the sea.
They saw a seagull
standing on it,
but they did not see Jeff and Kate.

They talked over their radio
to the people
in the Coast Guard motor boat.
They told them to come
and look for the children
in the water.
The motor boat came quickly.
It roared past the sailboat
so fast
the people did not see
Jeff and Kate sitting there
and sailing into the harbor.

They looked for Jeff and Kate
in the water.
But they did not find them.

Sadly, they started back
to the harbor.

But the sailboat
was already there,
and so were Jeff and Kate.
Mother and Father were
very happy to see them.
They cried and hugged
Jeff and Kate tight.

Then they hugged the woman
who had sailed them
safely to shore.
They hugged
the harbor master, too.
The harbor master called
the Coast Guard
to tell them Jeff and Kate
were safe.

Suddenly Jeff said,
"I know why I got seasick!
I got seasick because
I am so hungry.
I never had my lunch!"
So Mother and Father bought
hot dogs and lemonade
for everyone.
Then they all watched
people catching fish
from the dock
while they ate their lunch.

Ready for fun?

Don't miss READY-TO-READ HANDBOOKS like these.

IT'S MAGIC?
Written and illustrated by Robert Lopshire

"Fourteen fool-proof tricks requiring little practice and utilizing readily available material, explained in brief, easy-to-read text and explicit cartoonlike drawings."—A.L.A. *Booklist*

"...a sure way to mystify friends and entertain parents."
—*Kirkus Reviews*

DECEMBER DECORATIONS
By Peggy Parish / Illustrated by Barbara Wolff

Thirty Christmas and Chanukah decorations children can make all by themselves, "explained separately and simply for the youngest reader. ...Illustrations in green and black do a good job of explaining steps."
—A.L.A. *Booklist*

I DID IT
Written and illustrated by Harlow Rockwell

"Four children describe, in first-person narrative, their methods for making a paper-bag mask, a bean-and-seed picture, a papier-maché fish, a paper airplane, invisible ink, and simple yeast bread....this book's unusual approach...lends itself readily to independent work by young children."—A.L.A. *Booklist*

LOOK AT THIS
Written and illustrated by Harlow Rockwell

Three lively episodes containing complete, simply illustrated "how-to" instructions for making a paper dancing frog, delicious homemade applesauce, and a funny noisemaker.

YOUR FIRST PET
By Carla Stevens / Illustrated by Lisl Weil

"A pet care book that primary graders can read themselves. Short chapters describe the housing, feeding, and taming or training of gerbils, hamsters, mice, guinea pigs, goldfish, parakeets, kittens, and puppies. ...gives enough information for children to get started and adds important hints."—A.L.A. *Booklist*

"Parents...could do worse than make [this] book a required pre-requisite to that first pet shop purchase."—*Kirkus Reviews*

EVENING GRAY, MORNING RED
Written and illustrated by Barbara Wolff

"Primary graders are pleasantly introduced to weather through simple rhymes about clouds, sky color, the sun and moon, animals and birds, plants, and wind. Each selection is accompanied by a factual explanation of the scientific theory on which the rhyme is based."
—*School Library Journal*

"An informal, entertaining invitation to the subject."—A.L.A. *Booklist*